A VOYAGE CALLED LIFE

SHASHIKALA GADEPALLY

Made with ♥ on the Notion Press Platform
www.notionpress.com

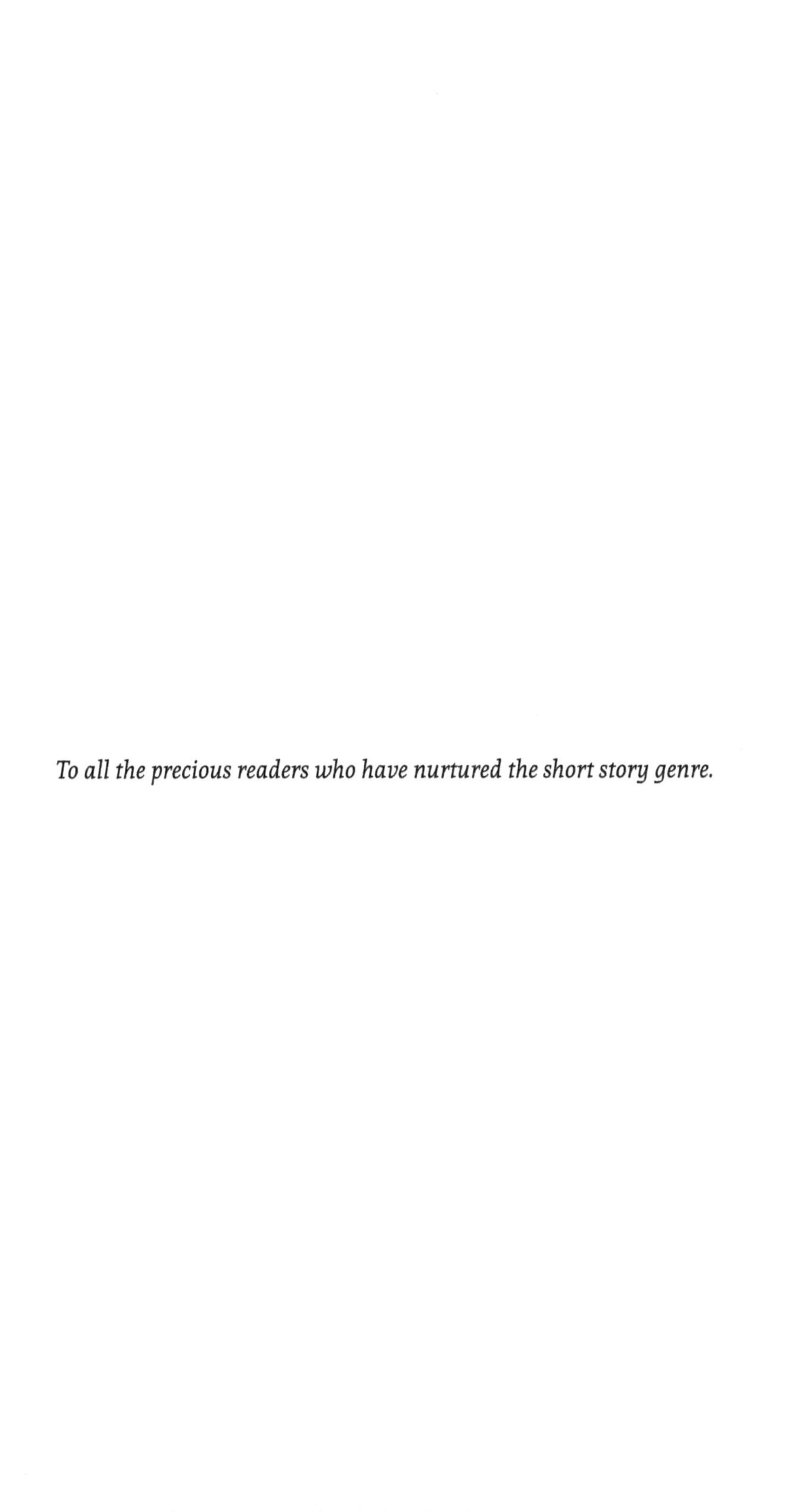

To all the precious readers who have nurtured the short story genre.

Contents

1

A Unique Love Story

"You look beautiful. The glow on your face is mesmerising. That skin texture - soft and supple makes me yearn for a touch. Your engaging looks are alluring. Hey! Don't get me wrong if I sound seductive; I mean to say you are irresistible." His eyes pricked my skin. I felt like hiding myself from his intent gaze.

"If looks could kill...." I could still feel the warmth of his eyes tickle my soft skin as I tried to turn away.

"Uff! His eyes are so intense...."

But my ego was too inflated to admit his charm.

"Look beautiful? I am beautiful. Isn't there a difference between the two?"

I snapped at him, trying to be casual and unruffled by his penetrating gaze. I glanced at him and caught my breath. I hadn't noticed before, but he was attractive in a unique way. His light pink skin, like that of a rose, was soothing.

Opposites attract - was turning out to be true.

He held my gaze. I could neither turn away my gaze nor keep it. He drew nearer and held me close to him. His proximity was tantalising. Was he enticing me deliberately to make me fall for him?

I jerked and moved away from his captivating aura. As I moved, his skin touched mine, which was an electrifying moment.

He pulled me towards him, and the jerky movement fused us.

His aroma touched my nostrils. He tried to balance himself and lifted me from the ground.

"That was unintentional, and don't read between the lines." He was defensive.

"I lost balance, too," I said meekly.

Looks locked, lips sealed, we stood in the market trying to figure out who should take the initiative to move away.

Someone called, "How much is 1 kg of potatoes?"

"Rs 40/- per kg. And, sir, don't bargain. This is the best season for potatoes. Do you see how fresh and sturdy they look? We must stand in queues in the big market and bid for one ton. Imagine our fate and that of the veggies when exposed to the sun. Our faces become dry and wrinkled. Sir, the softness is only skin deep; the yellowish-white interior is so hard and solid that nothing can affect its taste or colour. Not even this heat. Now, do you want to buy or bargain?" The shop owner's never-ending lecture on potatoes was jarring to the ear.

I looked at my companion. He chuckled as though he was enjoying the conversation.

I glared at him. The vegetable vendor had bared my traits in front of my companion.

How humiliating! All my tender feelings disappeared in no time, and I felt at a loss.

Did everyone know how versatile and accommodating I was? In an emergency, wasn't I the one who came to the rescue of the women in the house? Wasn't it me that readily jumped into the frying pan to tease the guests with my long, slender slices? Is there one person in this world who hasn't fallen for me?

Behind my humble appearance lies a world of mystery and adventure. Experimenting with me and exploring possible options, haven't the culinary artists fallen in love with me?

I have stood my ground during challenging situations. When a hoard of relatives invades your house, I have stood the test of time and have willingly become a saviour.

I deserve respect for my adaptability. Mash me, slice me, cut me, put me in gravy, fry me, deep fry me. I have served everyone with love and care. I appreciate how they value me. I have always been a favourite in inns, dhabas, restaurants, and star hotels. It makes me feel proud of my existence. Such a purposeful life! I am in love with myself. Self-love is no crime.

I was so lost in my thoughts that I failed to see my companion, my comrade, my love. With its intense aroma, the multi-layered Onion held me in a tight hug as though to comfort me.

"Isn't it strange that two of us, with such distinct traits, find solace and comfort in each other's company? You stand by yourself, but I need you to complete me. My loneliness is eternal, but when I am with you and others, I feel we all complement one another. Isn't it a fact that you are hard at the core, and I am soft and tender once the layers are sliced? I soften as soon as I am cut and put in a pan. You, on the other hand, take time to soften and yield to the heat. Opposites do attract, don't they?"

He tried to cheer me. I felt his warmth through his thin skin.

"I... am surprised at our texture and inner core. My outer layer is soft, but I am unyielding from within unless put under pressure. However, you are unique. Your hard surface melts in no time. My feminine elements are such a contrast to your male charm. You seem to hold so many mysteries within you; as the layers are peeled, you reveal your core, and your spicy scent stirs hidden emotions, just as it happened with me. What a wonder we have unravelled the mysteries deep in our hearts."

As I confessed my feelings, the vendor picked me up, weighed me, and packed me into the buyer's bag. As I slipped into the cloth bag, I felt my freedom disappearing into a dark void.

I wailed and whimpered but to no avail. I felt life sliding away from me.

Holding the bag firmly as he walked, I could feel my companion's tears trickling down his cheeks.

How helpless and desperate we both felt!

Would the curtain come down on our love story? Was it the END?

But every end has a new beginning somewhere else. Was it true?

ᐁᐁᐁ

"Onions are like gold nowadays. The prices have skyrocketed, but everyone in our family wants onions in every curry and salad. We buy only five to six kg of onions every month, and if I cut down on this one vegetable, so much commotion will be created as though the sky has fallen...."

She was muttering under her breath as she pulled out each potato and placed them in the basket.

I was elated; at least she was thinking of bringing us together.

But where are these onions?

Just as I was wondering, I saw another bag being placed on the kitchen counter. I felt satisfied in anticipation. We are destined to meet and stay together until the knife breaks us apart.

Ummm! That's a good one, I patted my back. I tried to peep from the basket. But the kitchen platform was too high to glimpse the bag's contents on the counter.

'Tcchh... can't wait to see my comrade." My eagerness grew along with insecurity.

I was pining for a glance.

What if I was sacrificed at the altar of the kitchen even before having a glimpse of my beloved?

No, no, no. The twain shall meet before any untoward incident happens. Fate cannot deprive me of my small pleasures. I have strived for this union. I was sure fate wouldn't let me down. I would get my share of joy. Well, I do deserve it, don't I?

But something was missing in this entire scheme of things. Was destiny conspiring against us? There were signs of it from the time we saw each other—love at first sight! But our separation was ingrained in our lives. Potatoes and onions were never placed beside each other; they had a logic—some gas from onions may react with my sensitive skin.

Separation was inevitable. But strangely, we blended well in some dishes. What a paradox!

My thoughts ran wildly. I was agitated.

Was Onion also restless thinking about me?

Am I the only one longing for a reunion?

And then it happened.

ᎭᎭᎭ

The light sound of the knife on the cutting board sent shivers across my body. Then, the pungent smell of the peeled onions, followed by tears in my eyes, cleared my vision. It wasn't the Onion that bled tears; it was me, the potato (not a couch potato). The tears tore my heart apart. I felt stifled and betrayed. I hugged my siblings and broke down.

The Onion had switched loyalties.

He was happily tossing in the pan with tomatoes and peas. The juicy, fleshy tomatoes, my partner in crime, too, had betrayed me.

O! Treacherous beloved, I shall not wail over split milk; I, too, shall find a partner.

I looked around, and from the fridge, spinach winked at me.

'Not forever, but we can be together and make the most of it. What say?"

Life did give alternatives and opportunities.

I blushed.

2
The Dawn

Hema tore the page, crumpled it and threw it into the wastepaper basket with loads of vengeance. The basket was already overloaded with the pages from her clipboard. Her knitted eyebrows, quivering lips, and shaking hands were proof enough of her mood. She ran her fingers through the long hair strands falling across her face. She pulled out the clip, binding her hair, and readjusted, bringing the strands into the hold. She stretched her limbs and closed her eyes. Her tired mind needed a break. This has been happening for the past two days. She couldn't pen her thoughts, not even a single word!

How disgusting! If anyone were to hear about this block, they would laugh at her.

'How she boasts about her creative skills and struggles with each word here.'

'Luck by chance. Best Selling Author indeed!'

'She might have bought her books to promote herself.....'

'Stop it, Hema, stop it. Let your imagination catch up with the story and not play havoc with your mind. Cool down, cheer up.....'

Exhausted, she slipped into deep sleep.

ppp

"Hema, can you hear me?' He bent forward and spoke in her ears.

It sounded as though the voice was coming from a far-off place. It was so faint and unclear that she thought she was imagining.

He repeated the question several times, which made her open her drowsy eyes.

The hazy figure stood before her, holding something in his hands.

'Oh God! A revolver? But why?'

Just as she was about to scream, he rushed to her and held her. To her relief, she saw a bouquet in his hands.

The fragrance of flowers tickled her nose.

With a jerk, she sat upright.

The tall, wheatish figure with broad shoulders looked familiar. But she couldn't place him. Did they work together? Was he her distant relative?

How did he get into her house at such an odd hour? It was past eleven p.m.

What was happening? Strangely, he was quite comfortable and trying to make her feel at ease in her own house!

She looked at him as though trying to place him.

Undeniably, he was charming. His charismatic personality was attractive.

She had to be cautious. She realised she was alone and pretty too.

Before she could get up and face him, he held her by hand and, looking deep into her eyes, offered her the bouquet.

'This is for you; the flowers are as fresh and fragrant as your thoughts and story ideas. You have a phenomenal narrative skill. The flow is like that of a stream. It cascades gently, flows unhindered over the rocks and boulders, manoeuvres skilfully, finds its path and moves. But have you ever thought of the potholes and plot holes in your books? The rhythm falters, the harmony disrupts, and the characters have no say in how the story twists and turns...." He paused with a heavy heart.

She was too shocked to utter a word.

Her mind went blank, and she felt as though she would faint.

"Wh.... who... are you?"

"Have you any idea what an author goes through? The struggles, challenges, criticism, trolling on social media, editor's demands, publisher's pressure. Life is not easy. It is not what the reader visualises. The harsh reality is hidden behind the facade. It is unpalatable."

Her voice croaked. What an ordeal it has been throughout her author journey. Her scarred memories were witness to it.

"Who are you, and what interests you in being here?"

She was frantic. Those pricks of conscience made her feel suffocated.

He was pointing out the loopholes that she had deliberately ignored. She knew about her bestselling tag. He would bare her secret in no time.

She knew she had no courage to face facts.

"What brings you here at this late hour?"

He was listening to her intently, savouring each word. It seemed as though he was revelling in her discomfort.

His silence was killing.

Then, at length, he broke his silence and spoke thoughtfully.

"I am that which you would never want to know. I am the truth behind your success. I have seen ups and downs in your characters, story plot, and marketing strategies....or should I say marketing goof-ups?" He was dangerously close to the truth.

Hema was too afraid to deny or stop him from spilling the beans.

How did he know so much about her? He was not even an acquaintance, though he looked familiar. He grinned, seeing her flushed face.

The target was hit.

"See, Mr...... whoever, whatever, you are intruding into my personal life. What I write and how I market my books are none of your business. If you wish to speak to me, visit my secretary. If dates are available, she will inform you. Now, just leave." Her tone was polite, though she was seething with rage.

This person knew too much, and he could spoil her reputation.

"Madam, reputation? Are you that innocent, or are you just pretending? What a glorious reputation madam has! And she believes it. Tcchhh. Sad, madam, really sad. Just peep into social media, you will know what people have to say about you. Your ideas are not yours; language and expression are borrowed/ stolen, and now AI is. When nothing is yours, do you genuinely believe you deserve 'name and fame'? There are hundreds of writers aspiring to be bestselling authors, but they are going the wrong way. What example are you all setting for the next generation? Chat GPT and AI tools are ruling the roost, nothing original, nothing natural.....” He broke down. His voice trailed off, and he fell on his knees, unable to control his sobs.

Hema was dumbfounded.

Was she being implicated in some author/book scam?

It was all baffling.

With her throat parched and limbs numb, she tried to reach for the water jug. Her hand quivered, and the jug dropped. It fell crashing on the floor, spilling water across the room.

He walked to the fridge, picked up a bottle and poured chilled water into a glass.

“Gulp it down, you will feel better.” His casual manner ruffled her further.

Breathing deeply, she addressed him, “You are smart and cunning. On the one hand, you soothe my troubled nerves; on the other hand, you subtly threaten me. From all this outburst, I conclude you are a reader who yearns for books of yesteryears and can’t relate to the most happening books of the era, mine being among those. I empathise with you.” Hema suddenly looked calm and at ease.

The haziness around him was clearing. His ranting about unfair dealings in author promotions, book marketing, and AI tools was falling into place like a jigsaw puzzle.

He was the protagonist of her upcoming novel, Charan.

Yes, Charan’s fiery personality was her creation.

But what was all this drama happening in her house at this hour?

What could all this mean?

She was still carving out characters, and the story arc faced ups and downs. She was unsure how to unfold the plot; it was all a rough draft.

Why was her character so agitated and pained?

What injustice has she done to his role and his character?

A storyline that has yet to take a definite shape undergoes several changes; the layered structure of a plot needs authentication, relevance, and validity. There's so much drilling that takes place before a character comes alive. What was he cribbing about?

Hema's mind was in a whirl.

He was not just referring to his character in the story but was criticising her for being unfair in her author's journey.

It shook her to the core. She felt broken and shattered.

ᑭᑭᑭ

"Raajan, I am unable to sell my books. Even our family hasn't reviewed them. They don't seem to have a good word for me or my stories. Not that I write for a livelihood, but it hurts when there are no buyers...." Raajan felt her pain.

"Hema, a book is valuable only when sold and gets comments, remarks, and reviews. You are not wrong in raising this matter. But tell me, what efforts have you put into promoting your book? Do people in our neighbourhood know you as a writer? You may not consider it a source of income, but what's the purpose of writing a book if it is not sold? It may sound harsh, but won't you feel good if you earn some money through your books? You are not being abnormally greedy; you are just being human." Raajan's persuasive skills were at their best.

Hema set off on a journey of self-discovery.

It was an intoxicating discovery that money was power, luxury and sophistication.

As her books rose on the chart, the bestseller tag initially filled her with pride and later arrogance. The fear of losing this charismatic fame drove her to compromise her integrity. To stay on top, she resorted to deception. She bought her books and distributed them to reviewers so they would put up excellent reviews.

She bartered her soul for a few reviews and loads of money. Her commercial success was thrilling, and there was no looking back.

Raajan devised strategies and handled publishers and promotional activities. As the author world learned more about her, interviews and book launches poured in.

She became desperate to maintain her ranking. Her stories gradually started losing their essence and punch. In her anxiety to retain her position, she began hiring ghostwriters who were well-versed in tools that were not beyond the human element. AI tools, Chat GPT, became HEMA the Author.

The human touch and emotion were fading, and this impacted the quality of the writing. Readers can't be fooled. A wave of protest swept across the book world. Lack of originality, receding emotions boomeranged, and Hema was impoverished. She had surrendered herself to the tinsel world. The intrinsic value of her originality was buried under glamour and money.

She is a commercial success but a human failure.

᠉᠉᠉

"Madam...."

Hema woke with a start.

There was no one in the room. The crumpled papers were strewn all around the waste paper basket.

She picked up the litter and cleared the bin.

Through the curtains, the first rays of the rising sun lit her room.

3

The Last Touch

Madhu felt someone tug at her dupatta. With eyes spitting fire, she turned to hit him. (Her thoughts were always filmy) There was no 'HIM', it was a 'HER'. Her cheeks were neither fluffy nor rosy, her eyes were not pools of love, her nose was scarred, and her hair was dusty and oily.

Madhu's romantic imagination was fractured.

She had imagined a young, handsome, macho man holding her dupatta to confess his love.

All her love thoughts came to nought.

'Chhhhh.... Leave my dupatta. How dare you touch my expensive dupatta.' She lifted her hand to slap the girl's dry, withered cheeks.

"Ammaaaa! "The girl screamed, shielding her face with both her hands.

Madhu noticed that a few old people were coming towards them. She held the girl's hand and winced at the smell that hit her nostrils.

"Uffff. Awful smell. Haven't you taken a bath?" She addressed the girl.

The girl nodded her head, "I haven't. I have no house, no family. I live on the footpath..."

"Ok, ok. I don't have time to listen to your filmy woes. I have better things to do."

The girl stared at her. She couldn't understand Madhu's annoyance.

"Madam, buy me something. I am hungry."

She clasped Madhu's hand and implored.

"Don't touch me with your dirty hands. My clothes will get soiled," Madhu murmured, fearing people would chide her.

"Please, mai.... I haven't had a morsel for two days. I am feeling giddy," the girl insisted. She didn't budge an inch.

Madhu felt trapped.

'What a girl! So insistent and stubborn. As though I owe her a meal.'

Madhu, born into an affluent family and educated abroad, never knew hunger pangs. The quantity of food that was wasted three times a day in their house could feed nothing less than five families in the slums.

Her lifestyle was triggered by all the fashion icons, models and advertisements. She carried with her an aura of sophistication and style.

Empathy or sympathy were foreign words for someone like Madhu, who had never seen poverty. Her annoyance and inability to resonate with the girl's needs were natural.

The little girl kept tugging at Madhu's dupatta.

She was as stubborn as Madhu.

'Had it not been for the function, I wouldn't have worn this behenji dress,' she grumbled.

Her car broke down just near the market, adding to her worries. When she was trying to find a way out, this girl barged into her private space and persistently bothered her. Madhu's patience (which was always quite low) snapped. Gritting her teeth, she jerked free from the girl's hold and walked straight into a handsome guy's arms.

'Hey, madam, careful. Not all falls are romantic.'" He winked at her—just what she was yearning for! She was too enamoured by his charismatic looks to deprive him of her proximity.

The girl stood her ground and walked towards them. Now, even better—awesome twosome! Her thoughts hovered around her little brother, who was starving and could not control his hunger pangs.

She had learnt to live with hunger as her companion, but not so him, the five-year-old.

She could deal with the rebukes of those she approached for some odd jobs but not with the heart-wrenching wails of her brother. Why weren't people kind? Why wasn't she considered a human being? Her desperation grew along with her. Her recent 'maid' work at the roadside hotel was also snatched away when a young lass struck a deal with the owner. Her innocent mind couldn't grasp the meaning of the unexpected change in the owner's attitude.

She was jobless and clueless, too.

On seeing Madhu get out of the car, her hopes were revived. She was beautiful and looked kind. Innocence personified. She was unaware that 'Appearances are deceptive'.

Madhu's dupatta was her sole rescuer, for it was close to her bosom. And she had heard that the heart is where feelings blossom.

What a paradox! Her heart beat for the handsome person holding her but failed to connect with the destitute.

Life's anatomy was complex.

"Mai... baba... just a little money will buy food for my brother."

Her words fell on deaf ears.

Madhu's romantic life had just begun on a footpath in the market, amidst the din of the vendors and in front of a poverty-stricken, helpless girl.

Why did Madhu's heart not feel for the needy? Why didn't that young man glance at that girl pleading to be heard?

Why's there such division? Why do some have so much and others hardly have any?

Life wasn't fair. Such imbalance!

The busy market had no time for these moral questions.

Madhu and the young man had no interest in delving into the social order or the question of fair, unfair, right or wrong. Some were privileged, and that's it.

The girl, in desperation, touched Madhu's little finger as though begging her to be kind.

The next moment, the girl's cheeks turned red with the imprint of Madhu's five fingers.

The slap was so hard that both lost balance and fell on the road.

The busy road became a pool of blood as a speeding van hit the girl.

Madhu, in a state of shock, could only recollect the girl pulling her as she fell.

She had touched her for the last time, but it was not to seek her help.

Time stood still.

4

Friends for Never.

Himanshu was angry. His inflated nostrils, blood-red eyes that spit fire, and clenched fists that wanted to punch that sneer away from her face spoke volumes of his rage. Could any human being be so harsh and insensitive?

Her attitude annoyed him. He was not the kind to take things in stride, so he felt he had a right to know about the sudden change in her manner. Weren't they best buddies? Then how could she be so nasty with him?

He got up and strode towards her. Her posture reflected her daredevil attitude.

She stood at the doorway, leaning against the glass door, her eyes mirthless. There were questions in her raised eyebrows and quivering lips. She clasped her hands as though controlling her emotions.

Was the sneer a way of hitting out at him?

He was bemused.

What brought her to his cabin in the middle of a meeting was a puzzle to him.

He was entrusted with meeting new clients, clearing their doubts, and resolving their issues. Customer satisfaction is the motto of any organisation.

Just as the meeting commenced, Reema barged into the cabin and demanded an explanation for some issue she was dealing with.

Himanshu was perplexed at this sudden outburst in the presence of new clients.

What opinions would they have formed about their bank?

It was an awkward moment for everyone in the cabin.

They excused themselves and went out.

Himanshu was left with the furious Reema.

In a taunting voice, she said, "Oh! So, the new person did not consider inviting me to this crucial meeting. I am struggling with those accounts that weren't tallying, and you promised to help me. The Manager, Shiv Prasad, tore me to pieces as though I had gobbled down the money from those accounts. I am a stand-by for someone in the Accounts department for a week, that's all. I am not usually the one that handles it. I am doing a favour. Instead of thanking me, he is...... How insulting! Doubting the integrity of an employee...."

Himanshu understood that her anger was not because of her boss' criticism but because he was responsible for new clients.

This new Reema was a revelation to him, and it wasn't a pleasant one. At the outset, she was amicable, compassionate, and supportive. He had often seen her helping the other employees with their complicated network issues, maintenance of balance sheets, etc.

Now, this ugly side shook him. Her jealousy was baseless, and her insecurity feigned.

"Do you even know how you messed up the situation? These new clients are the ones who can pull the bank out of the crisis it's facing. How juvenile! How can we repair this fractured situation? Moreover, ShivPrasad sir has entrusted me with this work, and he never mentioned that you, too, should be a part of the discussion. I can only decide things on my own if such freedom is given. You have put me in a tight spot."

Reema turned a deaf ear to his explanation. She continued to hammer him.

Himanshu stood his ground, and Reema hers.

He couldn't believe that Reema, known for her compassionate nature, was blunt and insensitive.

That was the beginning of the end.

ᗍᗍᗍ

Himanshu became nostalgic.

He remembered first meeting her in the bank manager's cabin.

He was awe-struck when she walked into the cabin.

She wasn't beautiful, but her poise was attractive. She carried herself upright and looked straight into the eyes. Some people may consider her audacious, but this was a sign of confidence and conviction for Himanshu.

The Chief Manager was unusually excited, which struck Himanshu as odd.

"Why is he holding her hand for so long? His handshake doesn't seem to end," Himanshu murmured.

"Meet Ms. Reema, Himanshu. She is joining our bank. Take her on a bank tour and acquaint her with the staff and work. She is in the Operations Department. Since she is new, you may have to guide her. Acquaint her with current/ongoing financial dealings, present clientele, and prospective clients. Is it okay, Reema?

Himanshu is one of the best in our operations Department. His precision and vast knowledge have won us many new clients. His support will take you places if you two work together like a team."

He felt flattered when he saw admiration in Reema's eyes.

"Now get going. I have a meeting to attend," The Chief Manager said, ending the meeting.

"This way, Ms. Reema," Himanshu was a little dramatic

She smiled and followed him. The welcome was heart-warming.

Her liveliness and cheerful demeanour won hearts, and Himanshu was no exception.

It was as though he had known her all his life, though it was purely workplace acquaintance.

They were not just colleagues in Global Bank but lived in the same colony and travelled together to their workplace in the same Metro. Their friendship grew leaps and bounds as time passed.

A hushed rumour was going around that Himanshu and Reema would announce their wedding date soon.

Their closeness became a sore in the eye for a few, but none dared to express it.

Shiv Prasad, the chief Manager, cautioned them that it could affect their efficiency and focus.

"Sir, I do not know the genesis of this rumour. Whoever has sparked this gossip has some secret agenda that could harm our bank's reputation. I would rather close my ears and focus on the upcoming meetings and our strategies to sustain existing customers and attract new ones. Unless our bank's financial stability goes viral in the market, it will be difficult to get new clients......"

Himanshu saw the manager fidgeting.

"Sorry, sir. I went overboard. I am trying to clarify things for you, that's all." He faltered.

"He smiled and said," I got your point. It's good to have staff like you who strive to bring more business to the organisation. Soon, there could be a meeting with the Executive Board members. There are a few issues that need to be addressed at the earliest. Nothing to worry about, but it's better to be aware of the organisation's present situation.

When Reema saw Himanshu come out of Shiv Prasad's cabin, she was jealous.

'What is cooking between the two? What's so important and urgent that Himanshu was taken into confidence and I have been ignored, right royal?'

The bug had bitten her, which was the turning point in their relationship. She never let go of any opportunity to taunt, ridicule, or call him Boss's tail. She was so consumed with jealousy that her attractive face lost its charm. Her vicious ways hurt Himanshu, but he was ready to make peace with her. She wasn't the one to reconcile or compromise—no, never. She had resolved never to trust anyone, not even Himanshu, who was once her close buddy.

Her suspicion grew. As time passed she felt that the Manager was favouring him and keeping her at bay.

ᐯᐯᐯ

"Sir, please clarify my doubt. It's genuine, and this is affecting my efficiency. Lately, I have observed that I am not included in any sudden meetings or decision-making. Have I gone wrong somewhere? Why am I kept aside?"

"... Or are you keen to know why Himanshu is often seen in my cabin, and you are kept away? Is that what bothers you, Ms Reema?"

Reema hadn't expected this direct, frank attack.

"I am sorry... sir."

"Now that you are here with your 'genuine doubts', let me clarify; in fact, I should ignore your allegations and insecurities, but since you have been a reliable employee till recently, I will tell you the reasons; firstly, he comes here to discuss the new strategies that he has come up with, secondly, I have permitted him to use the system in my cabin, till his desktop issues are resolved. Lastly, he is working with me on the existing clientele to check who can pitch ......" He paused as though he was reconsidering whether to reveal or to hold back.

"Yes, sir? Pitch... what, sir?"

"You may go now, Ms. Reema. Focus on more important things than nosing around... I'm sorry for that."

She dashed out of the cabin, leaving the door swinging violently.

Shiv Prasad took a deep breath.

"Uff. Like a tornado, she sweeps away everything, leaving traces of the remnants." He gulped down half a glass of water in a second.

"What information is she trying to elicit from us? And why is she so particular about clients? Is there something other than a healthy interest?" Shiv Prasad was not comfortable with this thought.

"I must check with the HR department about her references and previous workplaces."

It was so nagging that other employees who had put in more than two years of service in the bank had never crossed their limits or probed into matters not concerning them.

"She seemed to be a committed person, but she is turning out to be a nosy person." He thought aloud.

As he went around the counters, he noticed they were all engrossed in their work.

Reema was not in sight.

He peeped into the HR department to check if the HR manager, Ranganathan, was there. He was a senior banker, and he could help in this matter. It could lead to a significant disruption if anyone else came to know that he was trying to check on Reema's background after many months. It could also ruin his rapport with the other employees.

"Sir, are you looking for me?" The sudden voice from behind threw him off balance.

He turned and bumped into the person in question.

"No...no, not at all. You carry on." He hastened towards his cabin.

She strolled back to her desk.

🙙🙙🙙

Himanshu could not accept the incident, which shattered his peace of mind. All his hopes were pinned on the new clients, and Reema had ruined their chances of a revival.

What was her intention? Why was she behaving weirdly? Something was amiss.

'Let me talk to Shiv Prasad, sir. He might have already taken measures to resolve the issue.'

Before he could make up his mind, his phone buzzed.

"Sir, ... okay, sir. I will be right there." He rushed to sir's cabin.

Shiv Prasad sir was facing the wall and tapping his feet

. The cigar was shining, and smoke was spiralling from the pipe. Himanshu felt strange. Something was not going right in the room.

"Sir," Himanshu raised his voice.

"I have some news, and it's not good; it is shocking. It's about......"

"ME?"

Before he could dash towards the door, she pounced on him, punched him hard in the face and held both his hands in a firm grip.

"What are you up to, and where is sir?"

"What's the secret that you had come to share with him?"

"Secret? What are you talking about?" He tried to look casual, but his shaky hands gave him away.

He heard a groan from the restroom. He understood the situation and tried to reason with her.

"Reema, you can't escape. Two of us know what you are up to, so it's better to admit that you joined here only to ruin the bank's reputation and bundle the clientele to your organisation. Now we know why we suddenly faced a financial crunch, and the customers were complaining about our service not being satisfactory......"

He kept her engaged in conversation and quickly unlocked the restroom door. Lying on the floor gagged, hands tied behind, Shiv Prasad was in pathetic condition.

Hearing the commotion, the attendee rushed into the room.

She turned to run, but the attendee blocked the door.

Himanshu caught her and shoved her into the revolving chair.

She knew she was trapped.

"Confess." Himanshu's gentle tone was firm.

The attendee freed the Manager and gave him water.

Gasping for breath, Shiv Prasad sir said, "I suspected foul play and was about to call the police. She struck me and dragged me into the restroom. Rest, you know."

ᐳᐳᐳ

Reema's truth was hard to believe. She was a fraudster who had taken on such assignments for an organisation that targeted sound financial institutions.

There was neither regret nor remorse in her eyes.

"It's all in the game", were her words as the police took her away.

Reema's vicious smile haunted Himanshu for months.

5

Reversal

Seema looked at the tiny house opposite her bungalow. It had become a routine for her to watch the people trickling in and out of the house. She was fascinated by the people living in such a small, congested house that lacked ventilation and fresh air. There were no less than seven members who lived under the same roof!

Wow! What an adventurous life! Family is where people eat, sleep, play, quarrel and resolve their issues together. They were such a close-knit family!

'Oh, How I wish I were a part of that house! Day and night, I would have people around me. Grandparents, uncles, aunts, and cousins share their happiness, festivals, and celebrations. Ah, what fun it would be.' Seema yearned for those happy moments of a large family which would drive away her loneliness and despair.

She looked at her dress, which her mother had ordered from Amazon, which was as distasteful to her as bitter gourd. The soft, silky, body-hugging dress made her feel stifled. The multi-coloured embroidery at the hem and the neck looked gaudy. Though light pink enhanced her fair complexion, she had an odd feeling that it made her look like a buffoon. The embellishments and the contrasting colour combination made her feel uneasy. But her mother's choice and order had to be respected. There was never her choice, like or dislike.

Her wavy short hair was shoulder-length and trimmed to ensure it wouldn't grow below the shoulders. Her mother belonged to that fashionable circle of society that thrived on style and fashion.

Seema's highly successful businessman father hardly had time for the family. His high-profile business circles, social contacts, politicians, film fraternity..., and various circles bound his life. The four walls were a house, and neither of the parents could make it 'HOME''.

The connectivity, the bond that was so distinct in their lives, drew Seema to the house across the street. Their relationships manifested in every aspect of their existence. They were living a spirited, vibrant life, experiencing emotions, feelings, joys, sorrows, highs and lows as fate showered on them.

Seema could sense the deep emotional attachment of the family members as they shared the chores and shouldered responsibilities. She felt she was an integral part of that family, which adjusted to the vagaries of life, did not crib about lack of material comforts, and was accommodative and supportive. The distance between her house and that across the street had never separated her from that family. Distance never matters; what matters is the closeness of the hearts. And her heart merged with theirs.

The father, dressed in ordinary clothes and riding a bicycle, was a picture-perfect image for her. The mother, clad in a cotton wrinkled saree, the grandfather in Gujurati-style clothes and headgear, and the granny, with her head covered and a long veil, were typical unpretentious joint families. For Seema, they were the best live examples and role models of a happy family.

But her joy of watching them was always short-lived.

Her mother could never tolerate Seema going ga ga over that family.

"They are cheap, road-side people who lack class. They live and die in poverty. Look at those surroundings: unclean, muddy front yard, and how many people live in that hut-type house? What is so fascinating about those hunger-stricken morons? I fail to understand your feelings for them. The worst is you refuse to socialise with our circles. Look at Monica, Riya, Aashish and Anirudh; they go with their families for outings, mingle with their peer group, share their knowledge, and play together, and you are one odd one in the family and our friends circles. You will only understand the value of money, luxury, and affluence when lacking them. Her mother's preaching and complaints failed to move her. Nothing but an ordinary life could touch her heart. She resonated not with her family but with the one that presented life's value- four walls with a human touch.

ᗕᗕᗕ

"Seema, baby, why are you standing in the sun? Come in and play in your toy room. The sun is too harsh on your fair complexion, and you will get tanned. You know Mama doesn't like dark colours. Those dark circles around your eyes tell me that you are not happy. What happened? Shall I sit with you for a while?" Her nanny hugged her and led her into the toy room.

"Nanny, why doesn't my mom understand my loneliness and feelings? I feel caged and alone. It is like flapping my clipped wings; it is so futile. I want the little joys of life without pretension or artificiality. Will I ever enjoy moments of love and care?" Tears welled in her eyes, and she broke down.

Maria, her nanny, was speechless. She knew she was as helpless as the poor (rich) little girl sobbing uncontrollably right in front of her.

Amidst her sobs, she said, "Why can't we be like that family who live in that small house with no facilities but that binds them together? To be happy, one has to be rich?"

This was a query which needed an apt answer.

Maria could only pat her back to comfort her.

ᗕᗕᗕ

"Lakshmi, enough of looking at that bungalow, looking at it a thousand times a day and wishing you could switch roles with that pretty girl will not transform our lives. So let your feet be firmly rooted to the ground, for that is our ground reality." Jyoti's harsh voice cut through Lakshmi's reverie.

She sighed and continued to clean the utensils. Nothing could make the dented and worn-out aluminium utensils shine. Her rough and peeled palms were proof of this. However much she rubbed them, they would only get thinner at the base—no shine, no glitter, just like her life.

Lakshmi secretly admired the girl on the balcony across her house.

"Why does she stand in the sun and look at our worn-out house? Her beautiful dresses will fade in the hot sun. Though I don't have such fashionable clothes, I feel happy seeing her in various dresses. Good to see her in stylish outfits." She sighed.

Having completed the house chores with her mother, she sat down with her books. Exams were fast approaching, and if she didn't fare well in the annual exams, her parents would make her discontinue her studies and slog at home or wait for the right age to get her married off into another joint family.

"Oh, no, no, no! What an awful thought! Enough of 'lacking and scarcity' in life. I hesitate to ask Mai for a new dress; Bhai gets Papa's old, worn-out shoes, and Mom wears the same old faded synthetic(the only one Papa had for her ten years back) for any function or festival. Dada and Dadi keep coughing throughout the night; Papa can't afford a specialist for treatment. Why is life so unfair with some?"

The innocent girl in the faded house across the street stood in the sun admiring and envying the girl's fortune in the bungalow.

Fair and unfair, just and unjust are relative terms. Will a reversal of roles resolve Lakshmi and Seema's conflict?

Life is a bundle of paradoxes and conflicts.

ϷϷϷ

Is there a closure to their narratives?

Is the universe listening to them?

Some stories continue endlessly.

6
The New Era

Soham yawned and stretched for the fourth time after Meera, his mother, shook him half an hour earlier.

'Mothers seem to have only one agenda: wake up children early, even on holidays. 'With a chuckle, he remembered his friend Mohan's quip, 'for want of better work,' which universally applies to mothers.

He grinned, pulled the blanket over his lethargic head, and dozed off again.

Meera, with a ladle in one hand and tea in another, barged into the room only to find her lazy son dead to the world.

"Oh God! Please give me some respite from this imbecile. It's a holiday for everyone; even the maid takes two leaves in a month; for a mother, there is neither a holiday nor retirement. She remembered Jaya Bachanji's social drama, 'Maa retire hoti hai'. It happens only in dramas and films, nothing in real life.' Meera became pensive.

'I will retire from my government service at 60 or 62, they will felicitate me, give mementoes, appreciate my work commitment and finally write me off from their attendance register and memories too, but this 'homework culture will never change. When was the last time I slept till seven o'clock or did not prepare breakfast or meals? If my dear husband needs to relax, 'take a chill pill' types, why am I never off duty after office hours? 'Holiday-

A soldier is never off duty', I can connect to this movie title; it is relevant and apt.'

Meera's thoughts were focused and clear. She rarely got time to think for herself.

In the present times, when social media is agog with posts about self-love, mindfulness, and women's health, Meera and the like have to snatch a few moments to check their emails or WhatsApp messages or respond to calls. It was unfair on the part of the patriarchal society to keep women under their thumb and go around campaigning for women's rights. What an irony!

Suddenly, she remembered the purpose of her visit to her son's room. She put the teacup on the bedside table and ran down the stairs. The eggs in the boiler had burst open, and the kitchen was filled with the egg odour. She emptied the contents into the bin and put two more in the egg boiler.

"Ma, what are you up to? Can't you boil two eggs for your son? Much Ado about Nothing', Soham quoted Shakespeare.

Meera jumped in her skin at this unexpected voice that came from the door behind her.

She turned to find Soham and her husband standing at the door, enjoying her monologues and asides.

"You both scared the life out of me," she whined.

Mom, why were you carrying a ladle when you came to my room with tea? You haven't started cooking, right?" Soham was amused.

"And what is this Meera, grumbling about no holiday, no retirement? Women's empowerment asks you to empower yourselves with more energy, stamina, and better health to 'continue with your good work at home'. The world needs such committed human beings, I mean women. Am I wrong?"

Meera's eyes flashed fire.

"Eu tu, Brute.... Are you serious, Pratap Singhania? I thought you weren't the regular husband type. I credited you with more wisdom and sensibilities, if not compassion and empathy. No wonder our son, THE SOHAM, speaks in a condemning tone with me. He neither respects me nor values my work. At least I get paid for my services in the office; at home, it is an unpaid, full-time job with no even perks. You have disappointed me, husband Ji. Would you like this to happen with our daughter, who is completing her MBBS in a few months from now? And what kind of culture and values are you teaching to our son?"

Soham and Pratap were both stupefied at her outburst.

"And you, Soham, were awake and pretending to be asleep. Yes, as you said, I want better work. Let me take my 'me time' from this moment. It is only ME TIME. I will pamper myself, relax and enjoy my time. If you have one life, don't you think it applies to me, too? I will go out with my friends, apply for leave for as long as I want and go places. Any protest or objection from either or both of you is not entertained. I turn a deaf ear to both of you. Now, thank you for this awakening."

The finality in her voice was disturbing.

ᕭᕭᕭ

"Sir, I want to take off for a few weeks. I am planning a trip with my family. It is a surprise for them. I will complete all the pending work and hand it to Mr Rajan. I deserve a break from my routine life. When I resume work at the office and home, I will be doing more justice as an employee, mother, wife, and, most importantly, woman. After this vacation, I plan to take voluntary retirement to focus on my mission for quite some time......"

The firmness and determination in her voice made the Manager interrupt, "Is there any workplace issue? With your colleagues, management, work atmosphere and culture? A break from work is quite natural, but retirement is unthinkable. Could you please explain?"

The HR Manager needed to be more relaxed. It was like a sudden thunderbolt.

He had known her for over five years, and her work efficiency, skills, and knowledge were way beyond the fresh recruits. Her experience in various departments gained her seniority, and she was due for promotion.

Meera realised how shocking it must be for him to listen to her sudden decisions.

"Sir, don't get me wrong, but women let go of their small pleasures, compromising their health and peace. I have been reading about mindfulness, self-love, and women's empowerment, but all this is on paper, on social media, and in closed auditoriums. Sadly, it never reaches those women who are deprived of even the right to live. I have resolved to remove it from the closet and bring it into the open. This vacation is my first step in this direction. I know it is a big leap and one of its kind, but I know my family is with me in this venture."

Rudra Narayan, the HR manager, was proud to see Meera think of social work beyond office work.

"Madam, it is rare to see a change in perspective for oneself and fellow women. I appreciate your novel thinking and innovative ideas. It is refreshing to see our employees take a step forward."

My support and best wishes are with you always, madam."

Meera's colleagues congratulated her when she announced her future venture.

Though they would miss her lively interactions, everyone felt she was moving on for a more significant cause. Her female colleagues expressed their willingness to join her in her mission.

Feeling triumphant and proud, she headed towards her house.

❧❧❧

When she reached home, she found Soham and Pratap slumped in the recliner sofas. She went straight to the fridge, took a water bottle, and gulped it down. As the chilled water touched her throat, she felt refreshed. She knew both were watching her, but none spoke.

Her resolve not to give away the secret couldn't be contained further. She hid her smile and walked past them. Pratap caught her hand and held it in a tight grip. Soham stuffed a rasagulla into her mouth.

"Happy Anniversary to the best couple and parents." Soham hugged her.

Pratap made her sit on the sofa and brought a chocolate cake.

"This is for the most respectable woman in our lives who has dared to dream big. Congratulations for taking a big leap in life...."

"What?" Meera couldn't put two and two together.

"My dear maa, we know what happened at the office. This is the result that Dad wanted when he taunted and belittled you a week back. This master plan was to bring out the dormant Meera to the forefront."

Meera felt like dancing in joy.

"Don't stop yourself, Meera; you deserve to be honoured. Dance like you have never danced. No amount of cajoling and instilling confidence would have brought out the real you; the other day your outburst and anger against the injustice to women folk was an intended act from our side. It triggered the right emotion. Here we are celebrating the new you."

"How did you know?"

"I know your HR Manager. The past week has been quite a tense one for both of us. Your anger had not subsided, and you really took a break from the kitchen, something that has not happened even once in our twenty years of married life. So, I met your HR manager and briefed him about our comic interlude. He assured me he would inform me about anything happening in the office."

So, madam, what's the itinerary for our travel plans?"

Their vibrant smiles spread new hope, hope that envisioned a new era, not just for the deprived and the underprivileged but for women who were the backbone of the society.

7

Much Ado About Nothing

It was pitch dark when Sudesh reached home.

'These power cuts are getting on my nerves. The blazing sun during the day and power cuts in the night, what a deadly combination! Sun God is in revenge mode, and the electricity board is hand in glove with the sun.' His aside was as loud as an open dialogue

He searched his pocket for the house key but couldn't find it. In a frenzy, he took out his backpack and looked for the key; it wasn't there, either.

'Where could it go? It neither has wings to fly nor legs to walk away.' His annoyance peaked when he realised his mobile phone was missing. What in the world is happening? Is it some joke that fate is playing with me?'

His frantic efforts to remember the 'last seen' status of the key and the mobile met with a roadblock when his memory failed to trace the appearance of those two items.

"Hey, hey! What's happening to me? Cool, cool, cool. Don't panic. Take a deep breath, relax and then think." He calmed himself.

The street was still dark. None of the houses in the neighbourhood had generators, and since it was almost midnight, not even a lantern or candle was lit. The moon, too, had taken leave as it was the new moon phase.

'What luck! A bumper offer from nature, too.' With a wry smile, he started walking towards the main road. If luck favoured him, he would come across a street light.

Luck was now on his side. He had never experienced such delight or ecstasy before. The main road was illuminated, and what's more, there, in the corner of the street, stood a strong and sturdy PCO. The PCOs lost their prominence once mobile phones came into existence. The most often used, tall wooden boxes erected at every corner ceased to be necessary after the advent of the cell phone culture, which invaded people's privacy and peace.

Sudesh felt good fortune tagged along with him, as did the lights and the telephone booth.

His impatience grew when he saw someone in the booth. The phone conversation never seemed to end. He tapped on the glass door twice and waited with folded hands.

Not even in his wildest dreams did he think he would be standing at a phone booth so humbly one day.

Destiny has a way of putting humans in the right place. Today, Sudesh became the puppet.

It looked like an eternity when the person emerged from the booth.

Sudesh gave the person a nasty look and stepped into the world of telephones. As luck would have it, the call was not getting connected. He banged the phone, and it got connected. It must be like me, a Kickstarter.

Hello...he...llo ... can you hear me, Rakesh? Yes, it's me, Sudesh, calling from a public booth. Now listen to me. Did I leave my phone at your place? Or did you happen to see it anywhere? I don't know where, but it is missing. Oh, okay. It did not occur to me. I will do that right away." He slammed the phone and searched for his small pocket diary. It contained all the essential phone numbers.

He called Rakesh again.

"Hey, Rakesh, block my number or whatever the procedure is to ensure it is inaccessible to anyone who may find it. My life is at stake if it gets into the wrong hands. Meanwhile, I will complain to the police station. Do message me once. Oh no, what a dunce I am." He hung up and rushed to the police station.

The two town police stations were known for highly corrupt inspectors and constables. Without a bribe, no FIR would move an inch. But he had no choice; even if he had to bribe, he was prepared to do so.

ᗞᗞᗞ

"Babu Rao, there isn't a single bakra today. Who will do the bandobast for our chai-paani and dum biryani today? It's already midnight.

The havildar paced up and down, worried about the said arrangement.

The sub-inspector sat at the table, removed his shoes, stretched his legs on the table, pulled the cap over his face, and tried to get his share of sleep, which was always elusive to the police department.

Just as he was settling down comfortably, Sudesh rushed in and panted.

"Sss... Sir, I have lost my telephone diary. It's a pocket diary. I don't know whether I dropped it on the way home or someone flicked it from my pocket."

The sub-inspector and his staff gaped at him in disbelief.

"Come again... a telephone diary? Are you in your senses?"

Sudesh floundered again: "The lights were off, and I wanted to use the mobile torch. Then I realised the phone wasn't in my pocket or the backpack. Then I went to the PCO. It's such a blessing to have the PCO nearby..."

He gasped for breath, and the havildar helped him with a glass of water.

"Sir, sit for a while."

Sudesh closed his eyes and tried to arrange his thoughts and words.

"Sir, I have misplaced my mobile phone. It's an Android phone, I bought it recently. I need my phone desperately. Without it, I am crippled. All my data, contacts, and important information, oh, what would I do without it? Life looks deserted and abandoned. Can't imagine life without a mobile phone."

The sub-inspector himself felt breathless at this outburst.

"Sir, fill in this form and give all the details—yours and that of the mobile phone, the key features, version, etc. Once we trace it, you can come and collect it after verification. "His professional approach made Sudesh doubt the rumours about the police station and its bad reputation.

As he completed the form, he realised he was unaware of most of his phone's details.

"Sir, may I call my friend? I am unsure of some of these details I must fill in." He felt odd admitting the facts.

"So, you use it day and night and feel there is no life without it. Yet, the basic details of an instrument are close to your bosom, so you have to check with a friend! Wah, what an irony!"

The havildar and those in the lock-up laughed their hearts out.

Sudesh was too worried to pay attention to the mocking faces.

He called Rakesh and asked him to help him furnish the details. Rakesh, too, was at a loss.

"To he... with it. This Rakesh always uses my phone to call his girlfriend, talks to her for hours, makes my bill shoot up and never offers to pay even ten rupees; he cursed his friend, "Sir, I am unable to get the details. Is there any other way out? I have never felt so lost and desperate in my life."

The havildar said," Sir, if you can remember the store where you bought it, that could help."

The sub-inspector looked at him with appreciation.

"Ummm, you could do that. See, easy solutions to difficult problems."

Sudesh scratched his head. "Online purchase and all details are in WhatsApp and mail. Sir, may I open my email on your phone? That could be a solution."

"Okay, go ahead."

The network ditched him this time.

"Bad luck, dear sir."

Sudesh felt the universe was conspiring against him.

"Let's wait a while; network issues don't last long. (usually)"

Sudesh looked at his watch, "I wish I had synched my phone with the smartwatch."

"Sir, my network is restored."

"You may use havildar's phone."

"Did you install Google Find My Device on your mobile? It makes tracking easy. Ah, from the look on your face, I can make out a big NO."

The roadblocks to trace the phone were increasing by the minute.

As the police and Sudesh tried to resolve the challenges of finding the mobile, a miracle happened.

No, no, no. No good Samaritan walked in with the mobile phone.

A faint memory struck him.

"Sir, now I remember. Instead of putting it in silent mode, I switched it off while in a meeting, making it all the more difficult to track. What do I do now, Sir? It is an expensive one."

The sub-inspector felt a wave of sympathy for this troubled guy.

As a last resort, he checked the backpack once to rule out the possibility of it being in the bag.

"Give me the bag. Let's check it."

"Sir...... I haven't checked the backpack. How foolish!"

He unzipped all the compartments and emptied the contents on the table: documents, a tiffin box, an airtight dry fruit container, and all the paraphernalia required for his job—but not the phone or the key.

The secret pouch?

He pulled out the five-inch secret pouch from the backpack's hidden pocket.

The key and the mobile had caused such havoc in the narrow, dark realms of the pouch, ...like Adam and Eve in the GARDEN OF EDEN, after tasting the FORBIDDEN FRUIT.

Safety matters!

8
Bridging the Gap

The day began with breaking news. It is the new culture on News channels.

The news - Businessman Ankur Verma's new look.

New Channels vie with one another to grab the 'BREAKING NEWS', however trivial, irrelevant, and unnecessary. They resort to the worst strategies (tricks) to flash the news first so as to retain the top TRP.

The Vividh Bharati channel, run by Parameswaran, a retired government employee, always tried to bring authentic, genuine information to the masses. The public trusted the channel. Parameswaran's team neither asked for favours nor did favours. Their uprightness, sincerity and truthfulness made them the number-one News Channel in the country.

Hailing from a humble background, his miseries and struggles were endless. He imbibed his father's moral strength, which empowered him to face the challenges.

Parameswaran did not have any political backing or the kind of money needed to run a channel. His sole ambition was to present news that exposed the malpractices and unfair dealings in political, business, and education systems. If social order had to change, the mindset of the public had to undergo a drastic transformation, and he believed that could happen only when the common man rejected the small favours of the big elite.

He was an ambitious Channel owner; his ambition was to rekindle the dead human spirit. Complacency and acceptance without questioning were the bugs that infested society and the middle-class mind. He belonged to a middle-class family that lived and withered away without fighting or challenging the challenges. As a child, he experienced the pain of injustice and the fear of being banished.

His father's untimely death and his mother's dementia were all the result of his father's truthfulness and honesty.

A senior journalist in a reputed newspaper, Swaminathan's straightforwardness, daring, and fearlessness won him an equal number of friends and foes, which, over time, became fewer friends and more opposers. The rivalry was not a professional one; it was more of a political one. Political pressure increased as the newspaper gained prominence and became number one in the country. The publisher, Balwinder Chadda, was given two options: shutting down the business or dismissing Swaminathan from service.

Chadda knew the repercussions of going against the system. He apologised to Swaminathan while handing over the termination letter. Swaminathan wasn't shocked, for he knew it coming. His words were a tirade against the entire system. He voiced his strong opinion about the divide in the economic system, which was widening further. His articles were a powerful commentary on the malpractices rampant in law and order. Neither the gentry nor the business circles could withstand the might of the pen.

Swaminathan was a movement. Nothing could stop the tide of change lashing against the corrupt society's shores.

Despite being disowned by the newspaper, which was not just a source of livelihood but also a commitment he had made to himself, he started his own journal. Influential people from various walks of life, from industrialists to politicians, felt he was a threat to law and order and imprisoned him on charges of corruption, bribery, and revolting against the system.

His death was hushed up, and cremation was done in prison without the family's permission. Parameswaran was ten years old when he saw so much disorder in society. His silent resolve to bring justice to his family motivated him to complete his Master's in Journalism. He knew his chosen path would have a destiny similar to his father's, but that couldn't deter him from the righteous path.

Dealing with his mother's dementia, his father's untimely death, and his future wasn't easy, but his determination was rock-solid. He knew his goal and the road. Instead of joining a publishing house or a newspaper, he took up a government job. He required money to accomplish his ambition. He continued the government job until retirement, saving enough money to embark upon a journey into the media world.

ᗡᗡᗡ

"Paramesh Sir, why is our channel going ga ga over this news about Ankit Verma's new look? It sounds like a third-grade movie dialogue. We are here to set standards and streamline the media—print and e-media. Instead, we are focusing on insignificant information about businessmen and politicians. Have we forgotten our mission?" Harpreet Singh's concern was genuine.

Paramesh was engrossed in the news, which boosted the channel TRP. This is business, like show business; it thrives on the investors, and if the investment channels are closed, you and I will be on the streets, so relax and let the public bring money into our channel. If we have to grow, something other than what we have done in the past will work out. We have to keep idealism at bay and embrace practicality and reality. We will monetise the news if big money is involved in fake news. I know my moral stand, but I will go ahead with corrupt practices if they give me money to run my channel. I have to pay my bills and disburse salaries to my employees. Let us be honest in our dishonesty."

Harpreet saw a glint in Parmesh's eyes.

"Sir, I am with you. Sometimes, we have to reverse the situation to set things right." He sighed with relief.

The breaking news flashed through the day, and the public went wild.

'If you like this new look, press the green button....'

The more votes, the more the inflow of money. The advertising industry was ready for a makeover.

And his channel was ready to bulldoze the corrupt by being one among them.

His boss was not evil.

Parameswaran was very much like his father; he was practical. He cut the roots subtly.

Acknowledgements

Heartfelt gratitude to SHEROES- The Women Only Social Network, for continuous support and appreciation.

I would like to acknowledge the following authors:

Shakespeare for the title of one of the stories – Much Ado About Nothing

Eu tu, Brute from Julius Ceasar

'Maa Retire Hoti Hai – a TV show

Jaya Bachchan Ji's show

Author Bio

Shashikala Gadepally has embarked on a journey with her newfound passion for writing. Her creative urge and imaginative faculty have given her wings to explore the unknown realms.

She has authored several books in various genres, including fiction and poetry, with themes ranging from socio-political suspense thrillers to romance and human relationships.

Her favourite authors are P.G. Wodehouse and James Hadley Chase.

Her simple, lucid language enhances readability, and the easy flow of words connects the reader to the storyline.

Her eBooks published on Amazon Kindle are collections of poems on the relationship between nature and human beings, human relationships and the conflict between nature and man.

Her debut novel, The Absent Citizen, focuses on a civilised society in which social and ethical values have been neglected.

Her collections of short stories are Beyond the Horizon, Till Eternity…., The Untold Sagas, and A Twist in the Tale.

Her collections of poems are Verses of Life, Silent Musings, Waves and Petals, Symphonies - ruminations of Fragments and 'An Ode to Love', Living in Shadows and The Dark Realms.

She started her author journey at sixty, and there is no looking back.

9 798894 752358